For Kevin,
the man with
the pigeon hat

Henry Holt and Company, *Publishers since 1866*
Henry Holt® is a registered trademark of Macmillan Publishing Group, LLC
120 Broadway, New York, NY 10271 • mackids.com

Library of Congress Cataloging-in-Publication Data
Names: Stutzman, Jonathan, author. | Fox, Heather, illustrator.
Title: Don't feed the coos / Jonathan Stutzman ; illustrated by Heather Fox.
Other titles: Do not feed the coos
Description: First edition. | New York : Henry Holt and Company, 2020. |
    Summary: A cautionary tale in which a little girl must find a way to
    escape an insatiable flock of pigeons after sharing some bread with one.
Identifiers: LCCN 2019018802 | ISBN 9781250303189 (hardcover)
Subjects: | CYAC: Pigeons—Fiction. | Determination (Personality
    trait)—Fiction. | Humorous stories.
Classification: LCC PZ7.1.S798 Do 2020 | DDC [E]—dc23
LC record available at https://lccn.loc.gov/2019018802

Our books may be purchased in bulk for promotional, educational, or
business use. Please contact your local bookseller or the Macmillan
Corporate and Premium Sales Department at (800) 221-7945 ext. 5442
or by email at MacmillanSpecialMarkets@macmillan.com.

First edition, 2020
The illustrations for this book were created digitally.
Printed in China by RR Donnelley Asia Printing Solutions Ltd.,
Dongguan City, Guangdong Province

10 9 8 7 6 5 4 3 2 1

Don't FEED the COOS!

COO

Jonathan Stutzman

illustrated by Heather Fox

Henry Holt and Company • New York

When you see a coo,

you will be tempted

to give it a treat.

Coos are adorable,

peaceful,

kind of silly.

But Don't
FeeD the
Goo!

If you feed one . . .

COO

COO

COO

they will ALL come.

You will try to escape.

They will follow you

through
the park,

down
the street,

all the way **HOME.**

Your mother will not be pleased.

Wherever you are, they will be too.

At orchestra practice.

At the arcade.

Even at karate lessons.

Your sensei will not be pleased.

And to thank you
for feeding them, the coos

will
leave
poos.

Coo poos everywhere.

Coo poos covering everything.

You will lose your socks to the coos' poos.

Your backpack.

Your bed.

Your

mind!

All because you FED THE COOS.

You will do anything to make them leave.

Nothing will work.

You will try to hide.

But you cannot hide from a coo.

No matter what scheme you cook up,

your plans. Will. FAIL.
They will eat and eat and eat.
And coo and poo and poo on everything.

So just accept your fate.
Coos aren't so bad once you get to know them.

Give them names.

Knit them scarves.

Make them a part of your family.

Take them on
walks in the park!

Coos *love* the park.

A healthy coo is
a happy coo.

Yes! Feed them birdseed! Coos love food *more* than parks.

COO

MISSING PIGEONS

STAN'S SEEDS & stuff

You're getting the hang of this, kid!

Embrace your coos.

Because they will be YOUR coos 'til the very end.

There is absolutely, positively

to get rid of them.

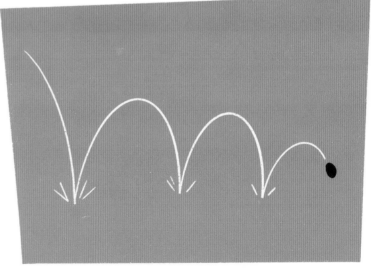

Clever child.
It looks like there
is a way . . .